DISNEY·PIXAR

INCREDIBLES 2

DASH'S

SUPER-SECRET
SUPER
NOTEBOOK

Written By:
Landry
Walker

studio fun
INTERNATIONAL

Faster than the fastest. More super than the most super. This is the story of the **MOST AWESOME HERO** that ever could be.

THE INCREDIBLE MASTER OF SPEED— THE DASH!

GLOVES
to keep from touching gross stuff

MASK
(None must know his true face!)

HIDDEN POCKETS
(for stuff and things!)

SUPER SHOES THAT AREN'T SLIPPERY
(important!)

Hi. So the other day I found Violet's diary and it was PRETTY BORING. Lots of stuff about boys and being all sad when they don't smile at her. There was pretty funny stuff about Tony Rydinger and kissing and some other boy, too, who sounded **EVEN DUMBER** than Tony.

But then Violet caught me in her room reading the diary, which wasn't fair at all because she was invisible. If she was visible, I would never have been caught! So it's really <u>HER FAULT</u> not mine.

Anyway, I figured I'd make my own book that's <u>WAY BETTER</u> than hers so that she can see how dumb her diary is (so dumb!). My book is going to be way better, because it won't be about kissing and mushy stuff. Instead, I will write about my amazing adventures and awesome crime-fighting skills!

BAM POW!

[P.S. This book is secretly about awesome adventures, but I've disguised it as a boring old math notebook (genius!). Violet will never figure it out!]

I have no idea what I am supposed to write in this.
I guess I could talk about my super-secret origin?
I mean, sure. Why not?

The adventures of the Amazing Dash began way back a little while ago when Mom and Dad tried to go off and have an exciting island superhero adventure without me or Violet.

So naturally, we hid on the jet mom borrowed, and soon we were on our way to the lair of bad guys.

Our plane was shot down, but that was okay. I KEPT MY COOL and helped paddle us across the ocean to the island.

Once there, I discovered the bad guys' missile site, blew up a bunch of stuff, and then rescued everyone. We flew in a motor home all the way back to the city, where we battled the GIANT ROBOT OF SYNDROME — some crazy nonsuper inventor guy that hated dad. He even tried to kidnap Jack-Jack. Luckily, he failed and now that I showed Mom and Dad how AMAZING I can be in a battle, they're sure to let me fight crime with them every day!

So . . . guess what?! Yesterday an ACTUAL super villain attacked!

IT. WAS. CRAZY!

He called himself the Underminer and he actually lives underground! He had a GIANT drill car and he was going to dig into the bank from underground. Luckily for everyone, the SUPER-AMAZING DASH was there to save the day. I mean, Violet and Mom and Dad and Uncle Lucius were there, too. (They helped...I guess.)

The drill was out of control, but we finally stopped it, and we barely wrecked any of the city. Violet kept trying to get me to hold Jack-Jack, but I was all like "no way," and then I was too fast for her to give Jack-Jack back. So . . .

LAYERS OF THE EARTH

NAME DASH

Pretend you are drilling into the center of the Earth. Write down the names of each of the layers of the earth that you would drill through.

Crusty Top layer buildings and stuff.

Tunnel layer Where bad guys hang out.

Subways and sewers layer.

Boiling hot lava layer.

The mantle is hotter than the crust.

T
(F)

The crust is the thickest layer of the Earth

T ?
F .

The inner core is solid

(T)
F

The outer core is solid

T
(F)

SCIENTIFIC THINKING

How do we know what the Earth is like if we've never seen it?
Volcano explorers use special fire proof submarines to enter the
earths core through active volcanoes. Once in the earths core, they take a lot of pictures
and they plant a flag letting all the other scientists know that they got there first.

Could anyone dig to the center of Earth and report back their findings?
Only the most awesome of super-geologists get jobs spelunking the earths core.
No one knows their real names though because they have to protect their identities
from the lava goblins that breath super hot molten rock at invaders.

Dash, please see me after class.

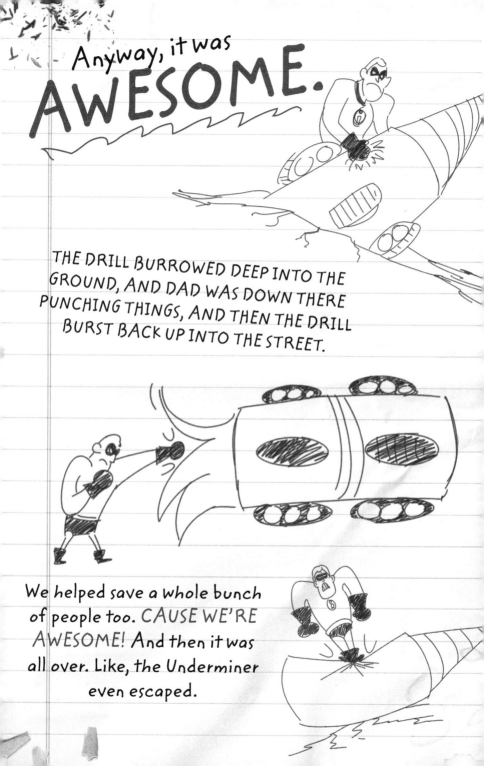

Anyway, it was

AWESOME.

THE DRILL BURROWED DEEP INTO THE GROUND, AND DAD WAS DOWN THERE PUNCHING THINGS, AND THEN THE DRILL BURST BACK UP INTO THE STREET.

We helped save a whole bunch of people too. CAUSE WE'RE AWESOME! And then it was all over. Like, the Underminer even escaped.

So then the police were mad at us and told us we weren't supposed to help anyone anymore.

HOW DOES THAT EVEN MAKE SENSE?

We're not the ones who wreck things.
THAT'S THE BAD GUYS!

Mom and Dad even had me create a perimeter to keep the crowds away from danger. I'd say that's a good thing, which means we shouldn't be in trouble for helping!

EVERYONE HAS THIS BLAME THING ALL WRONG!

BEING A SUPERHERO ISN'T ALWAYS AS FUN AS I THOUGHT IT WOULD BE.

I mean, the being a Super part is still really cool, but I kinda thought that after I helped save the city from the Omnidroid, then helped with the Underminer, mom and dad would treat me like I should be treated. Like one of them.

LIKE A REAL SUPER.

But instead all they seem to want to do is tell me to do my homework and not get into any trouble and all that stuff. I thought we were supposed to be a family now! Instead it's just more rules and more excuses and more hiding!

I hate hiding what I am!

So I'm not supposed to go and fight crime, and the police are telling us we have to behave and all that stuff, too. Okay, so I can't fight crime . . . in this city. But I'm really fast, and dad is really busy with Jack-Jack and Mom is getting to stop crooks, so I ran to a city where the cops don't know us!

I was hoping I'd find some super villains to fight there. But I didn't. I did get chased by an angry duck though. I've decided his name is Steve—the angriest Duck from planet Duckopolis.

HE'S MY NEW ARCHENEMY.

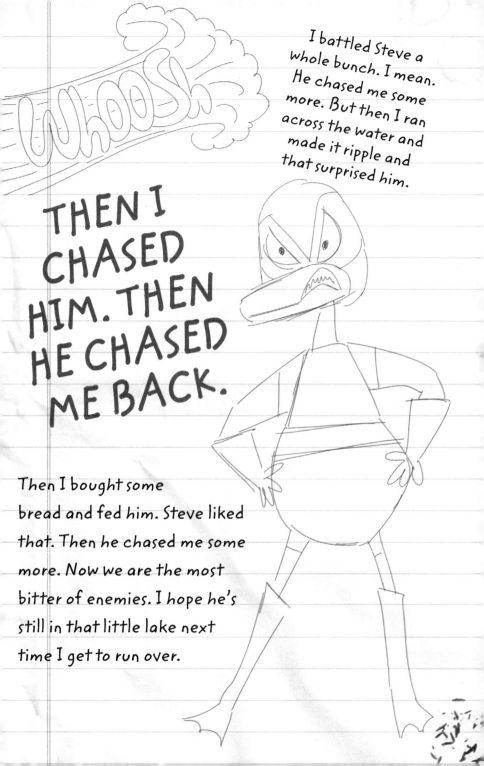

I battled Steve a whole bunch. I mean. He chased me some more. But then I ran across the water and made it ripple and that surprised him.

THEN I CHASED HIM. THEN HE CHASED ME BACK.

Then I bought some bread and fed him. Steve liked that. Then he chased me some more. Now we are the most bitter of enemies. I hope he's still in that little lake next time I get to run over.

Have I mentioned that we live in a motel now? Syndrome totally destroyed our house, so now we have to live at the Safari Court Motel. It's okay here. I can walk to the store and buy comic books, and they have these little airplane toys you can assemble. They're cheap too, which is good because I keep losing them.

I was sitting outside reading comics today when I got bit by an ant. It kept biting me, and I couldn't run anywhere to get away from it because it was already on me. ANT BITES HURT!

I wonder if there is a super villain somewhere nearby that's controlling ants. HE COULD TOTALLY BE WATCHING ME AND SENDING THESE ANTS TO BITE ME. I have to make a note to remind myself to see if there are any super villains nearby.

NOTE: CHECK NEIGHBORHOOD FOR ANT-POWERED SUPER VILLAINS.

MULTIPLICATION

NAME DASH

1.
```
   235
 ×  32
   470
  7050
  7,520
```

2.
```
   123
 ×  41
   123
  4920
  5,043
```

2.
```
   604
 ×  57
  4228
 30200
 34,428
```

3.
```
   704
 ×  98
  5632
 63360
 68,992
```

4.
```
   991
 ×  533
   2973
  29730
 495500
 528,203
```

```
   034
 ×  390
```

```
   195
 ×  585
```

```
   129
 ×  690
```

```
   430
 ×  316
```

```
   614
 ×  060
```

```
   1430
 × 2451
```

```
   4643
 × 2358
```

```
   2802
 × 1917
```

```
   2675
 × 1032
```

```
   2541
 × 1434
```

```
   2619
 × 1210
```

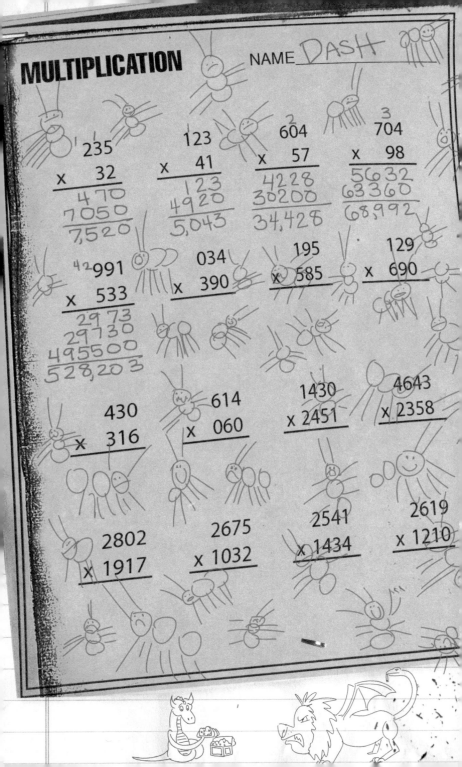

Mrs. Wallace says her real name is "Marta."
But I think it's a fake name. I mean, she's
WAY too evil just to be called "Marta."

AGH. I THINK MY MATH TEACHER IS A SUPER VILLAIN, TOO.

ALSO, I HATE MATH. Have I said that yet? Why do I have to do math when I have Super powers? It makes no sense! I'm not going to become some kind of math scientist! I'm going to stop crooks and criminals and save the world!

Math is not a Super power!

My math teacher's name is Mrs. Wallace, and she's clearly evil. She expects us to do a whole sheet of problems after school ... every day!

After school is when I run to other cities and stop crime from happening! How am I supposed to do math homework when I'm saving cities? I'm busy!

I've been running around
everywhere and there is no sign
of an ant villain in the neighborhood.
However, I did find millions and
millions and millions of ants.

IT'S LIKE THIS ENTIRE MOTEL WAS BUILT ON AN ANTHILL.

It got me thinking about the
Underminer. MAYBE HE'S IN
CONTROL OF THE ANTS? That
should have been my first thought. He
lives underground, and underground is
full of ants. Really, seems so obvious.
So maybe this invasion of ants is part
of his diabolical revenge plan? I tried
talking to Mom and Dad and Violet
about it. No one thinks that the ants
are under the control of anyone.

BUT WHAT IF THEY ARE?

We got a HOUSE!

Well it's not really ours. But we get to live in it because of mom's new job. She's working for these guys— EVELYN AND WINSTON DEAVOR— THEY'RE BILLIONAIRE INVENTORS THAT LIKE SUPERS.

THIS HOUSE IS CRAZY!

It's got remote controls and moving floors and hidden swimming pools and buttons and more swimming pools! I LOVE LOVE IT LOVE IT!

Anyway, it's pretty sweet having my own room again. But it's kind of weird knowing it's just loaned to us. But whatever... it's way better than the Safari Court Motel. I was like, why is it called the Safari anyway? It's just a bunch of sad people living in old smelly rooms without anything to do all day. Safaris are like, expeditions with jungles and tigers and monkeys. The hotel's name was a lie, and

I AM GLAD TO BE DONE WITH IT.

Lucius came over to the new house and showed me a new trick where he makes ice statue duplicates of himself.

I bet if I move fast enough back and forth I can make superspeed images of myself appear. I could probably even appear in two places at once by running back and forth really really really fast.

I'm going to try it now. BRB! ...

DIDN'T WORK. Crashed through door. BAD IDEA.

OUR NEW HOME!

DRAW A PICTURE OF YOUR HOME.

NAME DASH

What make it unique?
What does it have in common with other houses?

My house isn't really my house. It belongs to someone else. It has a river running through it and has a bunch of buttons that make the floor move around. It's really big and cool and stuff. I like living on a cliff, but it's kind of far up. We live really far away from other kids though.

The roof is pointy and looks kind of like an airplane.

It gets really windy on the mountain, so we don't use the deck much.

The river is cool, but you have to be careful of the deadly waterfall.

We used to live in a motel, and their were ants there. I didn't like the motel because it was small and it smelled really bad and there was no air conditioner. The new house is better. ~~Our house before that blew up when~~ we had to move because of usual normal reasons. Because.

AWESOME BACKYARD

Violet and I have a new game where I run across the yard and try to give her a high five before she can bring up a force field.

She's getting faster and faster with her shields!

I couldn't get across the yard before her shield went up. And bouncing off energy fields stings!

So we go out and I have these new cushion things in my shoes and suddenly she can't get her shield up in time. So I ran up to high-five her and the shield closed behind me, we were both inside the bubble! And I guess I had too much momentum.

So next thing you know, the energy bubble started rolling really fast and we kinda CRASHED THROUGH A FENCE.

AND ROLLED DOWN THE STREET. AND BOUNCED OFF A PARKED CAR. LUCKILY NO ONE SAW US.

OOPS.

So Violet got this idea on how to use the spinning energy shield as a pinball style attack. We did it kind of by accident once before when we were on Syndrome's island.

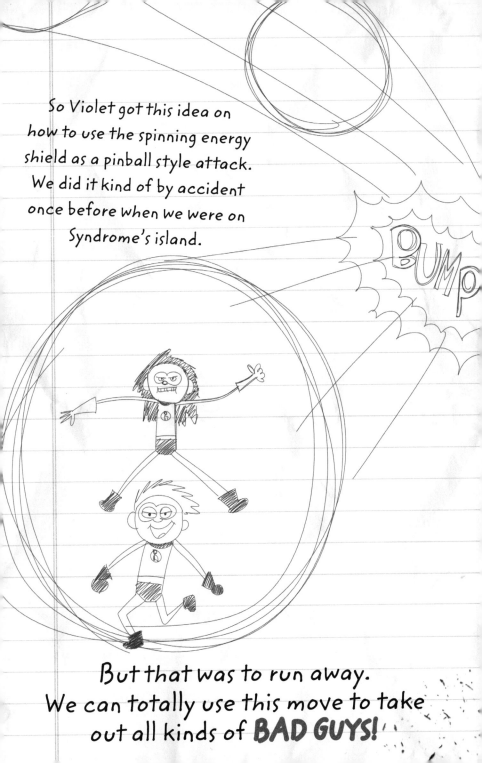

BUMP

But that was to run away. We can totally use this move to take out all kinds of **BAD GUYS!**

The Further Adventures of the Awesome and Super-Incredible Dash!

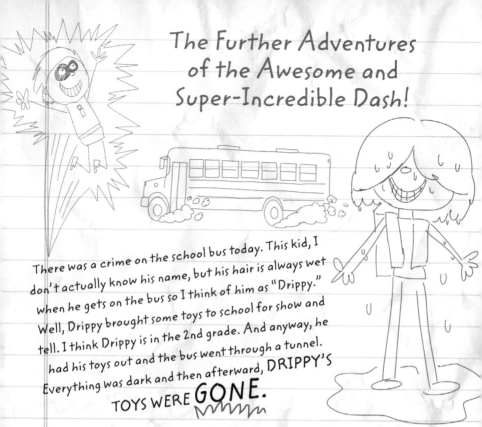

There was a crime on the school bus today. This kid, I don't actually know his name, but his hair is always wet when he gets on the bus so I think of him as "Drippy." Well, Drippy brought some toys to school for show and tell. I think Drippy is in the 2nd grade. And anyway, he had his toys out and the bus went through a tunnel. Everything was dark and then afterward, DRIPPY'S TOYS WERE GONE.

I HAVE TO GET TO THE BOTTOM OF THIS SINISTER CRIME. THE DASH IS ON THE CASE!

The bus ride today gave me more clues into the criminal workings of the villain I named the TOY TROUBLER! I used my super-speed vision to stare at everyone on the bus super hard. I mean, I guess I was just staring. I don't know that my eyes move at super speed really. I noticed that one kid looked extra nervous. He didn't bring any toys with him to play with, and lots of kids have toys on the bus. So was he trying to hide something? What's his story? I'll know more soon. I have a plan . . .

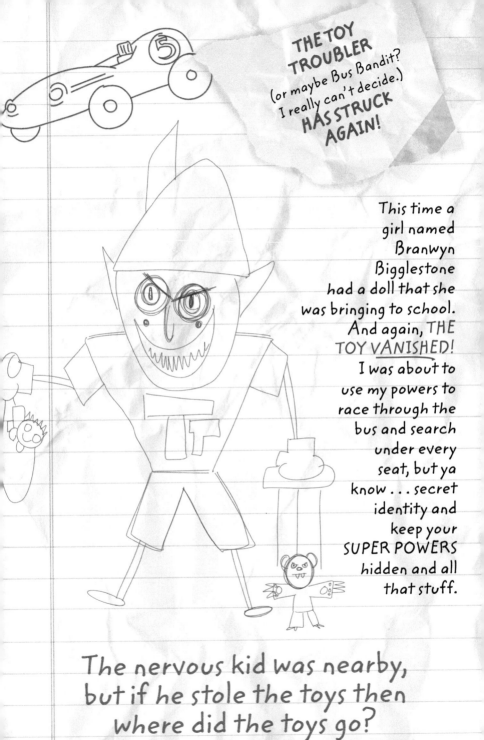

THE TOY TROUBLER
(or maybe Bus Bandit? I really can't decide.)
HAS STRUCK AGAIN!

This time a girl named Branwyn Bigglestone had a doll that she was bringing to school. And again, THE TOY VANISHED! I was about to use my powers to race through the bus and search under every seat, but ya know ... secret identity and keep your SUPER POWERS hidden and all that stuff.

The nervous kid was nearby, but if he stole the toys then where did the toys go?

AHA! Guess which super-awesome Super guy cracked the case? This guy! It was me! Cause I'm awesome!

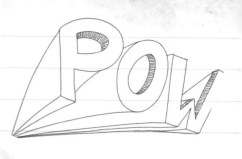

So it turns out the nervous kid is just really shy. His name is Joel and we ended up talking for a while. I feel bad, cause I was totally trying to see if I could get clues out of him so that I could reveal his identity as an <u>evil</u> villain. But he's just a kid, and I think now we might be friends. But the real villain has been unmasked and I have named him . . .

The Bus Driver of DOOM!

I thought it was weird how the toys were all disappearing from the front seats, but never the back seats. And how no kids seemed to have new toys. Then I noticed that the bus driver had a big backpack, and all the toys that were stolen were in reach from his seat. I followed him (like a ninja!) with a camera I got last Christmas and discovered that he was selling the toys!

I superspeeded the pictures onto the principal's desk and the BUS DRIVER OF DOOM was fired!
The toys are safe once more and the school bus is a nondoom place thanks to the super-sleuthing skills of...

I have to write a thing for school. They call it "creative writing," which sounds okay I guess.

I HAVE NOTHING TO SAY.

I just . . . they want me to write stories. But my life is way more interesting than stories. I asked if I could write about real things, and they said "NO!"

SO I HAVE TO MAKE SOMETHING UP. I DON'T LIKE THIS. IT'S HARD.

I'm so glad that's over!!!

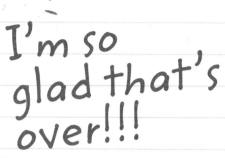

I finally just wrote my short story about planting farms and working with cows, and they said that was great.

Now I can go back to INTERESTING REAL STUFF like how I watched my mom on TV as she rode around on a motorcycle and punched muggers in the face! The newslady called it "charity work."

I DON'T GET THAT AT ALL.

SHE'S FIGHTING CRIME AND BEING TOTALLY COOL!

I snuck into Violet's room again. Her diary is still boring. She apparently has a date with Tony Rydinger tonight, and all she wrote in her diary is about how nervous she is!

All they're gonna do is sit and watch a movie! That's not hard to do! I bet she'll be all embarrassed when she sees him anyway, and she'll just turn invisible.

Or maybe they can talk about kissing, and crushes, and whatever.

She really needs a hobby!

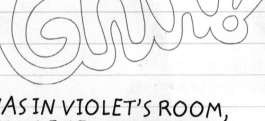

WHILE I WAS IN VIOLET'S ROOM, I TOOK ALL OF HER SHOES AND WRAPPED THEM IN PLASTIC WRAP.

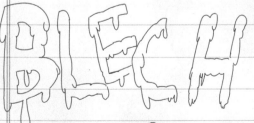

I made sure to do it after she was done getting ready for her date, so she won't see it until after. It will take her hours to unwrap them all.

Best. Prank. Ever.

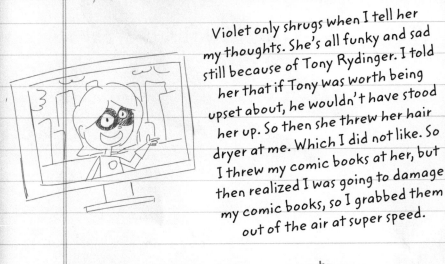

Violet only shrugs when I tell her my thoughts. She's all funky and sad still because of Tony Rydinger. I told her that if Tony was worth being upset about, he wouldn't have stood her up. So then she threw her hair dryer at me. Which I did not like. So I threw my comic books at her, but then realized I was going to damage my comic books, so I grabbed them out of the air at super speed.

Everyone says I'm too young to understand. But I think that's just what they say because I'm so obviously and totally right about stuff.

SMARTEST KID IN THE UNIVERSE

UPDATE: TONY RYDINGER IS A JERK.

He made my sister wait all night for him, and he never showed up, and now she's crying! I snuck out and was going to go yell at him, but I ran around the city for a full fifteen minutes and couldn't find him. I don't know where he lives.

Good thing for him.
I was mad.

No one makes my sister cry!

I unwrapped all of Violet's shoes before she saw them in the plastic wrap. I don't want to prank her right now.

FILL IN THE BLANK

NAME _DASH_

10 + __23__ + 97 = 130

__63__ + 95 + 26 = 184

104 = 32 + __40__ + 32

68 + __37__ + 34 = 139

52 = 20 + __13__ + 19

41 + 19 + __57__ = 117

55 + __56__ + 2 = 113

21 + _____ + 13 = 114

_____ + 34 + 88 = 175

18 + 48 + _____ = 129

143 = __66__ + 65 + 12

43 + 70 + _____ = 169

126 = 82 + _____ + 24

_____ + 41 + 19 = 136

_____ + 8 + 61 = 119

83 = _____ + 12 + 40

69 = 38 + 27 + _____

115 = __36__ + 75 + 4

77 + 28 + _____ = 185

Pffff! It's so frustrating! Mom is like, on TV and stuff and still we can't all go out and be superheroes?

She's running around showing off as Elastigirl, and I have to just go to school and be...nobody.

I mean, why should she get to have all the fun just because she's the adult. I have powers too! Dad says it's part of her job, fine great. But helping people is what I want to do. Why shouldn't I get to do that? I don't understand this world at all. None of this makes sense.

Maybe that's the key ... maybe none of this makes sense for a reason. Maybe it's all part of a super villain plan to divide our family and take over the city! Dad says I sound paranoid. But it's almost exactly what already happened to us with that Syndrome guy anyway.

THIS HOUSE IS SOOOOOOO BORING.

I HATE IT HERE.

I ran out of new comics to read days ago, and my airplanes all crashed and were destroyed. I took all the pieces and built a mega airplane with them.

IT WASN'T VERY GOOD. VIOLET HELPED ME A LITTLE. I THINK SHE FELT BAD FOR THROWING THE HAIR DRYER AT ME.

I'VE DECIDED JACK-JACK IS GOING TO BE MY SUPER-AWESOME SIDEKICK.

I will name him INCREDIBABY, and since he doesn't have any powers I will have to rescue him all the time. I asked him his opinion on this plan.
He said "gah!" which I am sure is baby for "you're in charge big brother—let's go fight some crime!"

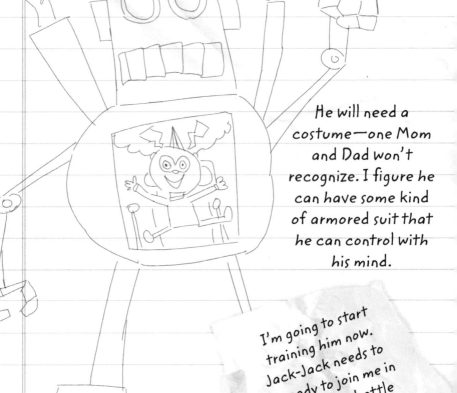

He will need a costume—one Mom and Dad won't recognize. I figure he can have some kind of armored suit that he can control with his mind.

I'm going to start training him now. Jack-Jack needs to be ready to join me in my one-man battle against injustice.

WELL...THAT WENT BADLY. I USED A BUNCH OF BOXES OUR STUFF IS PACKED IN AND BUILT A LITTLE MODEL CITY TO SHOW JACK-JACK HOW TO BE A HERO.

He crawled over City Hall, tried to eat the mayor, and had a... diaper issue (bleh! Stinky!) on the endangered townsfolk. Time to retire IncrediBaby.

Weird that some of the box buildings were on fire though. And another one looked like it had been chewed on by some kind of monster with really big teeth. I looked around a bunch to see if maybe the window was open and an animal had gotten in and...I dunno... lightning had struck?

THIS IS REALLY WEIRD. BUT AT LEAST JACK-JACK WASN'T HURT.

BYE BYE
INCREDIBABY

MS. MARTA THE MAD MATHEMATICIAN HAS STRUCK AGAIN.

Now she wants us to write our own math problems out. Like, she's the teacher! She should have to write problems out, not me. I'm just supposed to solve them, which is HARD ENOUGH ALREADY!

BRAIN GROW

DASH

I think maybe she's not really a math teacher?

I mean, what if she's not like even human? Maybe she's trying to use child brains to solve the equation that will get her spaceship working again? Maybe we're all just some kind of brain farm for her!

MUST INVESTIGATE FURTHER!

DECIMAL MULTIPLICATION

NAME __DASH__

0.66 x 0.001 = .00066   0.35 x 0.001 = .00035

176.3 x 0.1 = 17.63   6.25 x 0.1 = .625

0.918 x 0.001 = .000918   76.04 x 0.001 = .07604

0.019 x 0.1 = .0019   0.64 x 0.001 = .00064

3.86 x 0.01 = .0386   0.06 x 0.001 =

0.4 x 0.1 =   0.007 x 0.001 =

0.006 x 0.01 =   13.07 x 0.01 =

50.23 x 0.1 =   5.9 x 0.1 =

7.83 x 0.001 =   0.005 x 0.001 =

0.96 x 0.001 =   0.064 x 0.01 =

I TRIED TO ASK DAD FOR HELP WITH MATH. BUT HE'S <u>TERRIBLE</u> AT IT.

He does all the problems wrong. He thinks it doesn't matter cause he says the answers are right, but it matters if you do the problems wrong. So I don't get to be a superhero and my Dad can't help me with school and my Mom is always off fighting crime and we live in a house we borrowed from someone else.

Violet says Dad is under a lot of stress Which is really weird because before she was all

"Dad is the worst dad ever and he should stop being Dad!"

I guess it must be hard for Dad, he's used to being the one to go to work. And I really do miss Mom being around. I think I took her for granted maybe. She did everything and Dad is kind of out of his depth. Violet says it's good for Mom to be working. And I guess it is, but I wish she was also here, with us more. Or even better, if she'd just let us fight crime with her. I mean, it's not really fair that she hogs all the fun.

I wanted to go run around and see if I could find crime to fight in another city, but Dad ...I think he might be a little broken.

He's either sleeping, like, all the time. Or he's running around like crazy yelling about things. I think he's hallucinating. He even was muttering in his sleep about how there were lots and lots of little Jack-Jack's and that Jack-Jack was outside battling a raccoon. Admittedly, I heard a bunch of racket at one point. After Dad started yelling about this I looked around outside a little bit. There was a raccoon, it was glaring at me and it started yelling at me in whatever animal language raccoons speak.

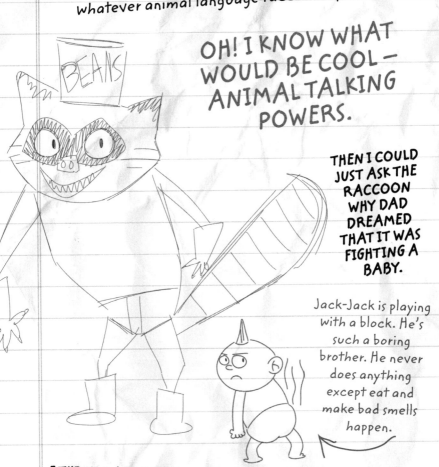

OH! I KNOW WHAT WOULD BE COOL — ANIMAL TALKING POWERS.

THEN I COULD JUST ASK THE RACCOON WHY DAD DREAMED THAT IT WAS FIGHTING A BABY.

Jack-Jack is playing with a block. He's such a boring brother. He never does anything except eat and make bad smells happen.

I THINK MAYBE ME AND VIOLET SHOULD WATCH DAD FOR A LITTLE BIT. JUST TO MAKE SURE HE'S NOT GOING REALLY, TOTALLY CRAZY.

Maybe I could get Edna to make me my own costume—something not Incredible.

If Mom and Dad are too busy to let us be a superhero crime-fighting family, I could go be a hero all by myself. I mean, I'm already doing that but I'm still wearing my matching family uniform, which feels weird without my family being there. So I should have like, a double secret identity.

I could even use a different name, like <u>Agent Speed</u>, or <u>Captain Zip</u>. Or maybe something else. . . . A supername has to be especially awesome. And that means I have to give it a serious amount of thought.

I ran to visit my archnemesis, Steve the very impolite duck. He was nicer today, probably because I brought crackers.

Then I ran out of crackers and he ATTACKED ME.

I've decided that now his super villain name is Doctor Duck, and that he is under an evil spell by one of the geese that hang out on the other side of the lake. Poor Steve the duck. It's not his fault he is cursed to be an

EVIL DUCK.

I thought maybe I could be a crime fighter in this other city. But I haven't found any crime. I mean, I guess that's good that there's no crime here. But it's really, really dull and I really, really want to fight bad guys!

Dad helped me with math?!
He like woke me up and
suddenly he can do math?

It was cool and all, but now I'm kinda worried? I mean
he couldn't do math and now he can. Is this somehow
connected to MRS. MARTA'S EVIL PLANS? I haven't
ruled out the possibility that she's an alien. She could
be one and no one would know because no one knows
what aliens really look like!

Maybe the math itself is
some kind of brainwashing
Super power.

Like if you learn the wrong equation—BAM!
You're under her math spells!

I'm going to try really hard
not to do any more math. Ever.

They had a career day thing at school where you have to try and decide what kind of future job you want. I thought it would be easy, since I'm going to be a superhero. BUT THEN I WAS LIKE, WHAT ABOUT MONEY AND FOOD AND BUYING STUFF? I think I need a secret identity job. And so I need to think about what kind of job I would want.

WE WERE GIVEN A LIST, BUT THEY'RE ALL BORING AND DUMB.

Things like "accountant" and "chef." I was thinking maybe I could be an archaeologist that specializes in superdangerous missions into pyramids, then I can fight mummies and scorpion monsters. Or maybe an astronaut and then I can defend Earth from aliens—

though running
super fast
without gravity
might be hard.

CAREER DAY

NAME **DASH**

Consider what your ideal job would be. Search through the career list below, and circle three different jobs you would like to have. Then write about what each job entails, and what you've learned in the classroom that would help you achieve these goals.

Accountant
Chef
Lawyer
Doctor
Police Officer
Scientist
Mechanic
Teacher
Dentist
Engineer
Salesperson
Plumber
Computer Technician
Veterinarian
Mummy Fighter
Time traveling space man
Old West cowboy

I think that I learned a lot about mummies and why there are lots of them in ancient Egypt from when we learned about ancient Egypt. I think that if mummies were to come back to life, the entire world would be in danger because mummies would be angry from being locked in pyramids. Because of these things, I think it would be a good thing to fight mummies.

We learned in class that different parts of the world exist in different time zones. So in some parts of the world it's today, and in other parts it might still be yesterday. I worry about this a lot, because time is obviously broken. How much more will it break? Dinosaurs were very real, and we don't really know what killed them. Maybe they are waiting to come through a crack in time? Someone must be ready. i can be that someone.

I liked when we learned about the old west and how everyone back then was really good at riding horses and finding gold. I think I could be an awesome cowboy.

I turned in my homework on what jobs I want and I was told I can't choose time traveler and that archaeologists DON'T fight mummy monsters.

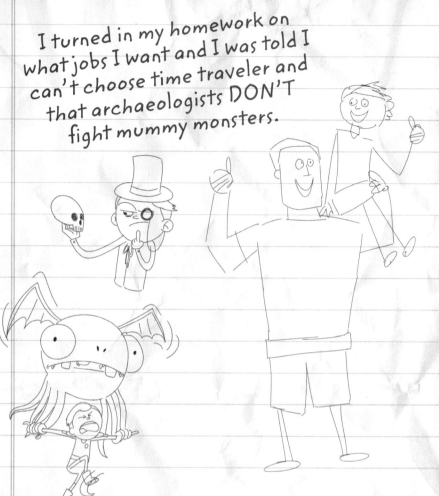

So apparently, I have to pick something else from the list and think about how it would be in "the real world." I don't want a job from "the real world." I want to be what I want to be, and I don't care what they say. I told Dad, and I thought he would be mad. But he agreed and told me I can absolutely be whatever I want to be and that he would tell the teacher that, too.

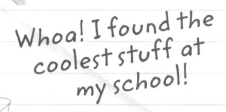

Whoa! I found the coolest stuff at my school!

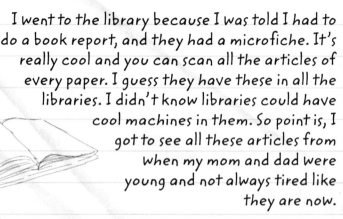

I went to the library because I was told I had to do a book report, and they had a microfiche. It's really cool and you can scan all the articles of every paper. I guess they have these in all the libraries. I didn't know libraries could have cool machines in them. So point is, I got to see all these articles from when my mom and dad were young and not always tired like they are now.

Dad used to patrol the city in his own special car—the Incredibile!

I CAN'T BELIEVE HE NEVER TOLD ME ABOUT IT BEFORE.

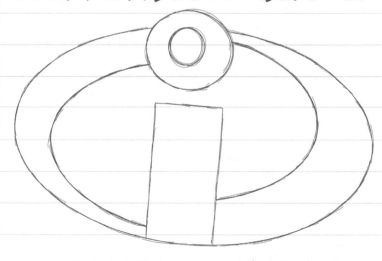

So mean. Anyway, he had his own car so he could get around places and find crime. I guess mom had a motorcycle back then. That's why she has a new one now. Violet said it's "nosetalsha." She says that means Mom is obsessed with stuff from when she wasn't old.

I kinda want a car.

THE DASHMOBILE.

But I'm faster than cars already. So I'm not sure yet.

Dad totally started to tell me about the super villains he used to fight!

He even had a vengeance squad attack him once, where all his enemies teamed up to fight him. He shrugged and said it wasn't that big of a deal.

Put two bad guys together and they just start fighting each other.

Mom came home and then Dad wouldn't talk about any of this stuff anymore. Told me not to repeat it and that he probably wasn't supposed to say anything because I might get ideas about fighting crime. But Mom IS ON TV! I can watch Mom fight crime on TV, but my own parents aren't supposed to talk about it!

Violet is feeling a little better and hasn't thrown anything in a while. I think it may be time to plan a new series of pranks. I thought I could start with a classic pie-in-the-face gag. It happens in cartoons a lot. I think I could build a contraption that would launch a pie from the wall when she puts on her slippers.

Other ideas:

Old Sock slapping contraption?

Toothpaste gun?

Cover everything in slippery butter?

Paint everything the exact same shade of green?

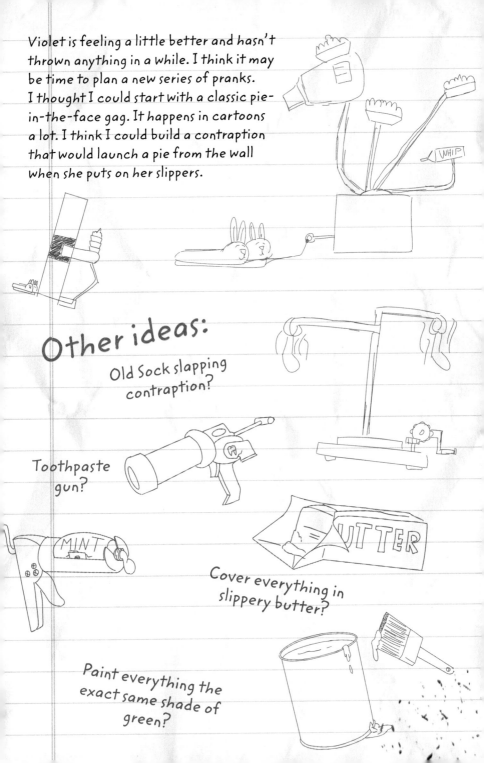

OH MAN!
NOW VIOLET'S <u>MAD</u> AGAIN.

So it turns out Tony didn't stand Violet up . . . not really.

Dad had his friends erase Tony's memory because Tony figured out Violet's secret identity, only they accidentally erased all memory of Violet!

I mean, that's pretty terrible, I guess. But Violet should be more careful!

Mom and Dad always say that our identities are our most valuable possession! I'm not surprised Dad erased his memory. Violet thinks Tony Rydinger is too "dreamy" to ever be an evil super villain, but I bet he's like, just one radioactive lab accident away from becoming her arch-nemesis!

HE'D PROBABLY
TURN INTO SOME
KIND OF SUPER
GROSS MUTANT
WITH NICE HAIR.

We're finally going to go somewhere for dinner!

Dad must feel really guilty about Violet because he's being super nice to her all the time. I dunno ... we get to go to dinner, so it all seems GREAT to me.

To be continued ...

Oh man!

That did <u>NOT</u> go well.

We went to Happy Platter across town, and Violet was all, "why are we going so far away?" and Dad was just "you'll see," and then our waiter was Tony Rydinger! And he still totally didn't know Violet! She was so mad she got up and left! Like she could really go anywhere. I mean, we were all the way across town, and it's not like she can run really fast.

Now she's in her room and not talking to Dad again. I was going to work on the pie-throwing machine, but I'm kind of afraid of Violet these days. She is MAD. She's so mad I think being mad might be her new Super power.

I was reading a bunch of old newspapers I found in the library about the old superheroes from a long time ago.

Gazerbeam and Dynaguy and Everseer and Psychwave and a whole bunch more. They had some wicked costumes and they worked in all these superteams like the Thrilling Three and the Phantasmics.

Supposedly a whole bunch of them went missing after Dad retired. Maybe they went into space to fight some galactic evil! I bet whatever it is, they're somewhere super cool doing awesome things that the dumb police of Earth wouldn't let them do!

I asked Dad, and he said he didn't want to talk about it. Anyway, Mom's getting to have all the fun. She even stopped a runaway train and has a new super villain called the Screenslaver. So unfair! I want a real villain, too!

3 DIGIT DECIMALS MULTIPLICATION

NAME DASH

1)
```
   13.4
 X    3
  40.2
```

2)
```
   12.1
 X    5
  60.5
```

3)
```
   24.5
 X    2
  49.0
```

4)
```
   12.6
 X    3
  37.8
```

5)
```
   10.1
 X    4
  40.4
```

6)
```
   27.3
 X    2
  54.6
```

7)
```
   17.3
 X    3
  51.9
```

8)
```
   21.1
 X    5
 105.5
```

9)
```
   32.4
 X    4
 129.6
```

10)
```
   18.4
 X    5
  92.0
```

11)
```
   52.7
 X    2
 105.4
```

12)
```
   23.8
 X    3
  71.4
```

13)
```
   51.6
 X    4
 206.4
```

14)
```
   65.9
 X    2
```

15)
```
   34.7
 X    5
```

16)
```
   42.8
 X    4
```

17)
```
   28.7
 X    3
```

18)
```
   75.3
 X    5
```

19)
```
   84.9
 X    2
```

20)
```
   54.7
 X    4
```

21)
```
   1.6
 X    5
```

22)
```
   37.8
 X    3
```

23)
```
      
 X    4
```

24)
```
   73.6
 X    4
```

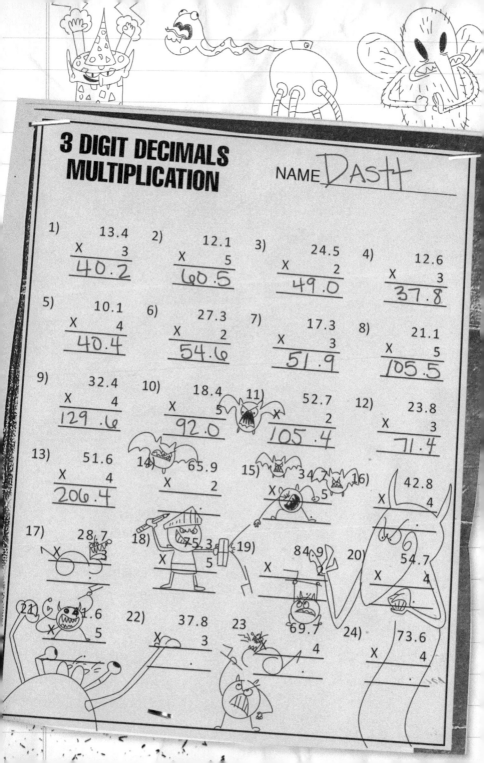

I thought math was BAD before, but now we're doing fractions and decimals and I think my life has become a living nightmare from which there can be no real escape.

IT'S
FOOTBALL!
SEASON!

Football tryouts are happening, and I am going to be the best and fastest football player ever! I am going to football the footballs the best. I will be hailed King Football and all other football players will bow down because of how awesome I am.

Dad even said I could play, as long as I play fair and don't use my speed. I used to think that was kind of dumb, but now I guess I see the point. I mean, it's not everyone else's fault they don't have powers. I shouldn't show off and make people feel bad. I wouldn't like it if that happened to me.

Football tryouts are today! Football tryouts are today! Football tryouts are today! Football tryouts are today! Football tryouts are today! I'm gonna play some football, and everyone's gonna be in awe of my football greatness!

Woo!

"THE DASH"
#1

update:
I did football tryouts.
Without powers it was
way harder than I
thought it'd be. I didn't
make the team.
I HATE TODAY.

Jack-Jack has powers!
Jack-Jack has . . . like
ALL THE POWERS!

HE WAS CHASING VIOLET AROUND AS A RED MONSTER AND SHE WAS SCREAMING AND IT WAS SO FUNNY, AND THEN HE SNEEZED AND <u>EXPLODED</u> THROUGH THE ROOF AND THAT WAS A LITTLE LESS FUNNY. AND THEN HE FLEW! MY BABY BROTHER CAN FLY! I MEAN, THAT'S REALLY COOL AND ALSO SO NOT FAIR!

I want to fly, too!

He also turned into metal and exploded into like, several smaller Jack-Jacks. It was absolutely the weirdest and coolest thing I ever saw.

DAD IS SO OUT OF HIS LEAGUE ON THIS. BUT HE WON'T CALL MOM TO ASK HER FOR HELP. INSTEAD WE GOT HIM TO FINALLY CALL LUCIUS. HE'S GONNA COME OVER AND TALK SOME SENSE INTO DAD...

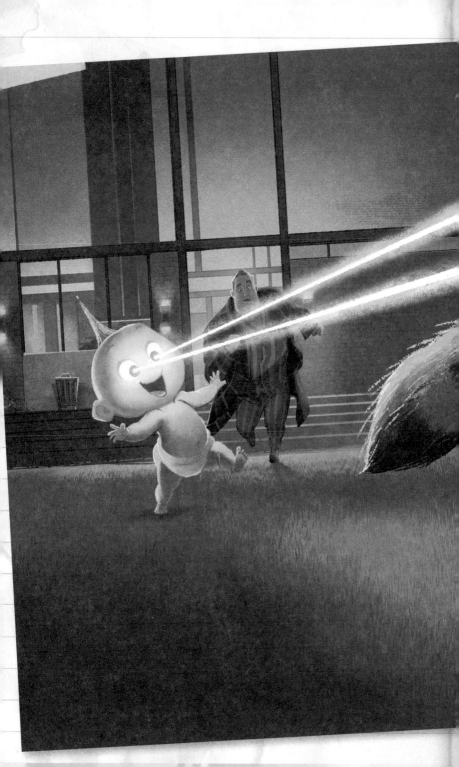

...THEN GET READY TO GET POWERED UP WITH MY NEW POWER PROGRAM!

EACH ONE WEEK COURSE IS DEVISED BY EXERCISE GURUS FROM ACROSS THE WORLD! WANT TO KNOW HOW THEY BUILD MUSCLES IN EUROPE! OR HOW THEY GET IN SHAPE IN JAPAN?

UNLOCK YOUR SECRET POTENTIAL AND BRING OUT YOUR HIDDEN STRENGTH! USE METHODS THAT HAVE BEEN PROVEN WITH INTERNATIONAL SCIENCE TO GUARANTEE THAT YOU NEVER HAVE TO BE WEAK AGAIN! EVER!

55kg

TIRED OF BEING WEAK AND PUNY? THINK YOU HAVE WHAT IT TAKES TO BE A REAL POWERHOUSE?

DAD TOTALLY FLIPPED OUT!

I think he's having some kind of midlife crisis. His old car was on TV and he started shouting and stuff. And then things went really crazy. Dad started digging through the boxes, looking for the remote control to his super car. He started pressing buttons on it and the thing came to life right on the TV. Dad said the car even launches rockets! I wanted to see the rockets in action, but Dad grabbed the remote from me before anything cool could happen. He was pretty mad, but calmed down eventually.

I HAVE ALL THIS STUPID HOMEWORK AND STUFF, AND I DIDN'T MAKE THE FOOTBALL TEAM. NOT THAT IT MATTERS. I'M GOING TO BE A SUPERHERO AND FIGHT ALL THE CRIME.

DETENTION SLIP

PERIOD/TIME OF DAY 2nd Period

STUDENT'S NAME Dash
CLASS Math
TEACHER Mrs. Wallace

1. The purpose of this notice is to inform you of a diciplinary incident involving the student.
2. Please note the action taken by the teacher and the corrective action initiated today.

REASON(S)_ FOR THIS NOTICE:
- ☐ BULLYING/HARASSMENT
- ☐ DESTRUCTIVE TO SCHOOL PROPERTY
- ☐ ELECTRONIC DEVICE
- ☐ LITTERING
- ☐ UNCOOPERATIVE/DEFIANT
- ☐ CUTTING CLASS
- ☐ DISRUPTIVE BEHAVIOR
- ☐ FIGHTING
- ☐ EXCESSIVE TALKING
- ☒ OTHER _Running in halls_
- ☐ CHEATING
- ☐ EXCESSIVE TARDINESS
- ☐ LEFT GROUNDS WITHOUT PERMISSION
- ☐ UNACCEPTABLE LANGUAGE

ACTION TAKEN PRIOR TO NOTICE:
- ☒ REVIEWED STUDENT'S FILE
- ☒ HAD CONFERENCE WITH STUDENT
- ☒ CONSULTED COUNSELOR
- ☐ CHANGED STUDENT'S SEAT
- ☒ DETAINED STUDENT AFTER SCHOOL
- ☐ TELEPHONED PARENT

PARENT ACTION AND RECOMMENDATION(S):
- ☐ STUDENT REPRIMANDED
- ☐ PARENT CONFERENCE RECOMMENDED
- ☐ STUDENT WILL MAKE UP TIME
- ☐ STUDENT SUSPENDED
- ☐ MATTER REFERRED TO _____
- ☐ OTHER

Mrs. Walla[ce]
ACTION TAKEN BY

DETENTION SLIP

STUDENT'S NAME Dash
CLASS Science
TEACHER Mr. Blake

PERIOD/TIME OF DAY 4th Period

1. The purpose of this notice is to inform you of a diciplinary incident involving the student.
2. Please note the action taken by the teacher and the corrective action initiated today.

REASON(S)_ FOR THIS NOTICE:
- ☐ BULLYING/HARASSMENT
- ☐ DESTRUCTIVE TO SCHOOL PROPERTY
- ☐ ELECTRONIC DEVICE
- ☐ LITTERING
- ☐ UNCOOPERATIVE/DEFIANT
- ☐ CUTTING CLASS
- ☐ DISRUPTIVE BEHAVIOR
- ☐ FIGHTING
- ☐ EXCESSIVE TALKING
- ☒ OTHER _Doodling on Workbook_
- ☐ CHEATING
- ☐ EXCESSIVE TARDINESS
- ☐ LEFT GROUNDS WITHOUT PERMISSION
- ☐ UNACCEPTABLE LANGUGE

ACTION TAKEN PRIOR TO NOTICE:
- ☒ REVIEWED STUDENT'S FILE
- ☒ HAD CONFERENCE WITH STUDENT
- ☐ CONSULTED COUNSELOR
- ☐ CHANGED STUDENT'S SEAT
- ☒ DETAINED STUDENT AFTER SCHOOL
- ☐ TELEPHONED PARENT

PARENT ACTION AND RECOMMENDATION(S):
- ☒ STUDENT REPRIMANDED
- ☐ PARENT CONFERENCE RECOMMENDED
- ☐ STUDENT WILL MAKE UP TIME
- ☐ STUDENT SUSPENDED
- ☐ MATTER REFERRED TO _____
- ☐ OTHER _____

Mr. Blake
ACTION TAKEN BY:

I don't need math OR football.

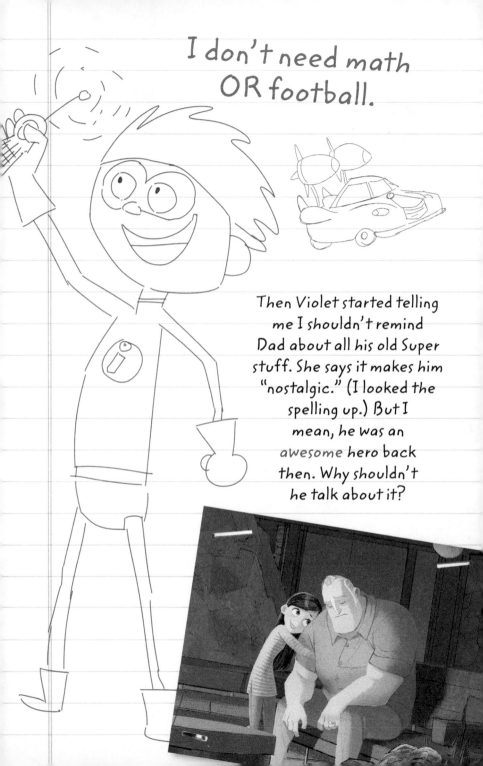

Then Violet started telling me I shouldn't remind Dad about all his old Super stuff. She says it makes him "nostalgic." (I looked the spelling up.) But I mean, he was an *awesome* hero back then. Why shouldn't he talk about it?

School today is SUPER dull. All we're learning about is poetry and stuff. I'm supposed to write a poem about my life. I'm not even allowed to have a life, let alone write a poem about it. BUT WHATEVER. So I'm writing in here pretending to write a poem.

You know what, maybe I'll actually write one. Here goes:

MY NAME'S DASH.
MY DAD HAS NO MUSTACHE.
I LIKE TO RUN REAL FAST,
AND AT PARTIES I'M A BLAST.

Boom. Poem done. 100% me.
I am the best.

I just decided I'm going to visit Steve the Duck today. He probably misses me.

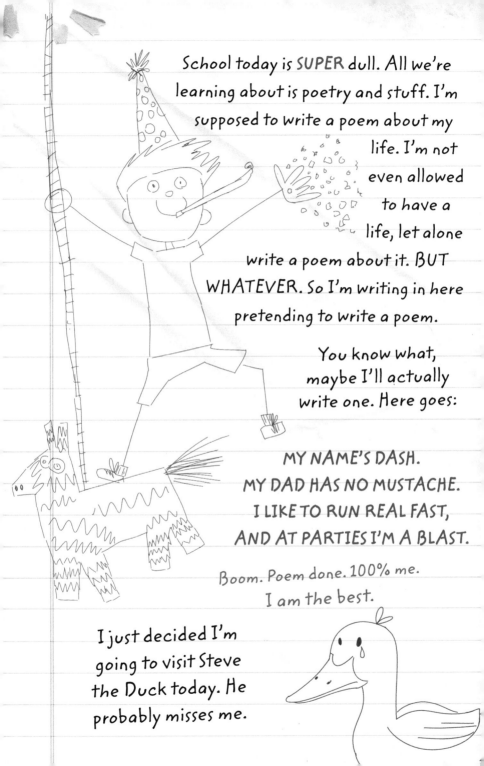

Since there is no superhero doctor guy out there to give me new powers, I was thinking maybe I could make my powers even better. I could train. That's what athletes do and they get better. So I should do it, too.

I drew up my own training plan. It starts with me running. I haven't figured out what else I should do yet.

"OH NO! I HAVE GAINED FROG POWERS. BUT AT WHAT COST?!!"

HOW I WILL TRAIN:

1. Run, lots.
2. Jump around.
3. Get faster.
4. ??

Dad dropped Jack-Jack off with Edna Mode. Either Jack-Jack will destroy her or he will come back to us as the most fashionable baby ever. Anyway, Dad passed out. I'm poking him with a pencil right now and he is just snoring and snoring and snoring.

He's been asleep for hours.

Can he even feel a poke with a pencil though? Bullets don't hurt him. So how can he feel a pencil if bullets don't even hurt?

I WAS GONNA ASK HIM IF HE EVER FOUGHT ANYONE FROM THE MOON. HE PROBABLY DID, BACK WHEN IT WAS COOL TO BE A SUPERHERO. NOW, IF THE MOON GANG ATTACKED, I'D PROBABLY HAVE TO STAY AT HOME AND EAT MY VEGETABLES.

Bleh!

I didn't find Steve the Duck. I think Sorcerer Swan might be up to something though. I watched him from afar, and he swam, like, a whole bunch. But that doesn't make him innocent.

There was a trail of crumbs that I thought might be a clue, but they were just crumbs.

This town seriously has no crime. I guess it probably does, but never when I'm around. My luck is terrible. I mean, can't somebody just rob a bank? Like maybe now would be a good time for aliens from the Moon to attack. I could fight the Moon Gang and they would all wear bubble helmets and carry ray guns. Then I could fight real Super villains!

I FOUND STEVE! HE WAS SLEEPING IN A DIFFERENT POND. SO I KIND OF WOKE HIM UP AND HE CHASED ME AGAIN. GOOD OLD STEVE....

Dad tried helping me with math again. But this time it was kind of cool. He made each problem into a story, and it all kind of became a game. Like, I have to solve the math problems to stop these bad guys that have guns and stuff, and when I do solve the problem, I make the bad guys explode. Dad made it like a Super power. It was fun.

DAD ACTUALLY MADE MATH FUN.

Whaaaaaat? Does this mean I've been mesmerized by the evils of Mrs. Marta's math magic?!! Teachers are the scariest kinds of super villains because they literally get inside your head and change your minds about stuff!

Sinister!

I GUESS IT'S KINDA COOL THOUGH.
I MEAN, MAYBE MATH IS OKAY.
See, I can't even believe I just wrote that!
I don't even know who I am anymore!

Note to Self: Is math cool?! Or am I being mind controlled?

DIVIDING FRACTIONS

NAME _DASH_

1) $\dfrac{3}{7} \div \dfrac{2}{3} = \dfrac{9}{14}$

2) $\dfrac{5}{9} \div \dfrac{1}{8} = \dfrac{40}{9} = 4\dfrac{4}{9}$

3) $\dfrac{4}{5} \div \dfrac{4}{9} = \dfrac{36}{20} = 1\dfrac{4}{5}$

4) $\dfrac{5}{11} \div \dfrac{2}{3} = \dfrac{15}{22}$

5) $\dfrac{3}{15} \div \dfrac{2}{9} = \dfrac{27}{30} = \dfrac{9}{10}$

6) $\dfrac{1}{10} \div \dfrac{3}{15} = \dfrac{15}{30} = \dfrac{1}{2}$

7) $\dfrac{6}{7} \div \dfrac{10}{3} = \dfrac{18}{70} = \dfrac{9}{35}$

8) $\dfrac{12}{5} \div \dfrac{4}{5} =$

9) $\dfrac{11}{9} \div \dfrac{3}{7} =$

10) $\dfrac{5}{2} \div \dfrac{7}{9} =$

11) $\dfrac{5}{8} \div \dfrac{9}{10} =$

12) $\dfrac{9}{7} \div \dfrac{3}{4} =$

I found an old newspaper article about how to get stronger and faster and build more muscles. The guy in the picture had muscles _everywhere_! I'm totally gonna do that. It said it's just a 3-week exercise program that's supposed to be <u>super</u> <u>easy</u> to do.

ADDING FRACTIONS NAME DASH

MORE

$\frac{2}{5} + \frac{1}{5} + \frac{1}{5}$ $= \boxed{\frac{4}{5}}$

$\frac{7}{20} + \frac{3}{20} + \frac{9}{20}$ $= \boxed{\frac{19}{20}}$

$\frac{1}{7} + \frac{3}{7} + \frac{2}{7}$ $= \boxed{\frac{6}{7}}$

$\frac{2}{8} + \frac{3}{8} + \frac{2}{8}$ $= \boxed{\frac{7}{8}}$

$\frac{5}{17} + \frac{2}{17} + \frac{3}{17}$ $= \boxed{\frac{10}{17}}$

$\frac{5}{22} + \frac{7}{22} + \frac{9}{22}$ $= \boxed{\frac{21}{22}}$

$\frac{25}{107} + \frac{70}{107} + \frac{5}{107}$ $= \boxed{\frac{100}{107}}$

$\frac{8}{45} + \frac{14}{45} + \frac{12}{45}$ $= \boxed{\frac{34}{45}}$

$\frac{3}{27} + \frac{8}{27} + \frac{14}{27}$ $= \boxed{}$

$\frac{1}{6} + \frac{2}{6} + \frac{2}{6}$ $= \boxed{}$

THIS MATH CLASS HAS LASTED LIKE, YEARS!!

I think that Mrs. Marta the Evil Mathematician must have teamed up with an evil clock villain or something. Why? Because she's evil! And she knows that making us sit here longer and longer is TORTURE!

So math is way easier and more fun now. But still . . . I wanted to go practice and get faster speed and more powers. But instead I'm stuck doing homework.

THIS CLASS IS TAKING FOREVER!
Ms. Marta keeps looking at my paper and shaking her head and giving me evil scowling eyes. It's not my fault that math isn't as fun as being a superhero!

Tic Tic Tic

The clock is moving sooooooooo slow. I just want to go to run and run and run. Class ends in ten minutes. But it's ending in ten minutes forever and ever. It's like this clock doesn't even move!?

TIME . . . IS . . . SLOWING . . . DOWN . . .

I did . . . the exercises . . .
so many . . . exercises . . .

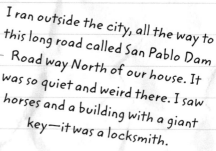

I ran outside the city, all the way to this long road called San Pablo Dam Road way North of our house. It was so quiet and weird there. I saw horses and a building with a giant key—it was a locksmith.

I had hoped it was a super-secret villain headquarters. Anyway, I kept going and eventually reached the dam. There was no one around, so I swam a whole lot! That's what the exercise thing said to do. I swam up and down and back and forth. Then I dried off by spinning and that made me dizzy. Then I ran home.

I don't feel like I have a whole bunch of new muscles. Really disappointed.
I put in a whole day's work!

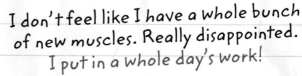

I'm still totally excited about football, but the teacher said that means I have to do extra good in everything else. How is that a thing??

Anyway, Math is easier now, but history is still super dull. Why don't we learn about dinosaurs? They're historical, and they're way more interesting than memorizing the Constitution. Dinosaurs didn't even need a constitution—they just ate stuff and stomped things. THEY ALSO DIDN'T HAVE TO GO TO SCHOOL.

All they had to worry about was meteors and becoming extinct—which admittedly went bad for them.

"Four score and seventeen million years ago . . ."

This day is sooooooo long . . .

There's an opening on the football team, and because my grades are better, they said I could tryout again!

I CAN FOOTBALL!

WOOP!

I'm still not gonna use my powers. I'm gonna play football and be the best, all as a normal kid—well, normalish. I mean, I'll have to try really hard not to be too fast or too slow.
But it's worth it!

FOOTBALL! YES!

WOW. JUST . . . WOW . . .

I went back to see Steve. I brought
lots of crackers so he wouldn't chase
me. He didn't. But I guess Steve
isn't really Steve. I mean, he is.
But he is actually a she,
and she has a whole
bunch of baby ducks now. I guess
her name can still be Steve. I mean,
why not?

STEVE IS A REALLY GOOD NAME!

I named her babies JoJo, Tweedles, and Marbles.
There's a fourth baby duck, but she's mean like
her mom. So her name is Lil' Steve.

I gave
Steve extra
crackers to
share with
her babies.

I gave one to the evil swan, too. He was
pretty nice. I decided his name was Nina
because it's also a good name.

MIXED FRACTIONS

NAME DAST4

15/15

1. $3\frac{1}{2} \times 1\frac{4}{7} \times 1\frac{1}{3}$

$22/3 = 7\frac{1}{3}$

6. $4\frac{1}{2} \times 3\frac{3}{4} \times 2\frac{2}{3}$

$= 45$

11. $1\frac{4}{5} \div 4\frac{1}{2} \times 1\frac{?}{?}$

$= 18/35$

2. $3\frac{1}{2} \times 1\frac{1}{7} \div 1\frac{1}{4}$

$16/5 = 3\frac{1}{5}$

7. $2\frac{5}{7} \div \left(1\frac{8}{11} \times 1\frac{2}{3}\right)$

$= 33/35$

12. $2\frac{1}{4} \times 1\frac{4}{11} \div$

$30/11 = 2\frac{8}{?}$

3. $1\frac{1}{3} \times 1\frac{5}{7} \div 1\frac{3}{4}$

$64/49 = 1\frac{15}{49}$

8. $2\frac{1}{4} \times 1\frac{2}{3} \div 1\frac{1}{2}$

$5/2 = 2\frac{1}{2}$

13. $6\frac{2}{3} \div 3\frac{1}{3} \times$

$28/9 = 3\frac{1}{?}$

4. $1\frac{1}{4} \times 10\frac{1}{2} \div 1\frac{1}{2}$

$35/4 = 8\frac{3}{4}$

9. $2\frac{3}{4} \div \left(1\frac{1}{9} \div 2\frac{1}{2}\right)$

$99/16 = 6\frac{3}{16}$

14. $1\frac{2}{9} \div 2\frac{1}{2} \times$

$= 11/12$

5. $1\frac{3}{4} \div \left(3\frac{2}{3} \div 3\frac{1}{3}\right)$

$35/22 = 1\frac{13}{22}$

10. $2\frac{1}{2} \times 2\frac{4}{7} \times 1\frac{1}{9}$

$50/7 = 7\frac{1}{7}$

15. $5\frac{1}{2} \div \left(1\frac{1}{2}\right.$

$10/3 =$

GREAT

I told Violet all about Steve the duck. She got irritated because we're not supposed to be superheroes. She said I had to stop or she'd tell dad. I went back anyway and said bye to Steve and Tweedles and JoJo and Marbles and Lil' Steve.

THEY ALL HISSED AT ME AND THEN THEY ALL CHASED ME.

I guess maybe Violet is kind of right. I don't want to get caught just because I'm sneaking out to hang out with mean ducks that don't even like me.

Dad brought Jack-Jack back. I'm wondering if now that he's got all these crazy powers, if I should revisit my plan to make him my sidekick.

I mean, he makes things kind of smelly, but he is my brother. We could probably be a pretty amazing crime-fighting team.

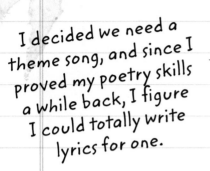

I decided we need a theme song, and since I proved my poetry skills a while back, I figure I could totally write lyrics for one.

"WHO'S THE HERO THAT'S LIGHTNING QUICK
AND WHOSE BABY BROTHER
IS HIS SUPER-POWERED SIDEKICK?"
"ZOOM! HIS NAME IS THE DASH
AND YOU BETTER NOT STOP HIM
OR YOU MIGHT GET CRASHED!"

[It's a work in progress.]

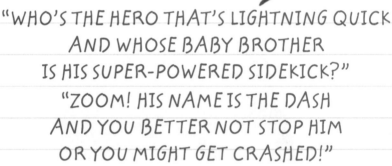

Dad said that I can't fight crime with a baby. I think he's underestimating Jack-Jack. He's a baby, yeah. But he's a really really really strong and easily angered baby. I WOULDN'T WANT TO FIGHT HIM.

But Dad did say that when I'm a little older he would take me out on patrol and teach me a few things. He said having a sidekick is a good idea he should have thought about more seriously a long time ago. Dad's a little old to be my sidekick. I guess it's okay though...

I don't want to hurt his feelings by telling him that.

And we have this cool tracker tablet now that we can use to see where Jack-Jack is when he uses his powers.

He can vanish into some other dimension and we can still find him. He also splits into multiple babies and the tracker warns us! Edna is really cool to have built all this stuff. Maybe I should have talked to her about helping me get more Super powers. I'm going to have to remember to do that. . .

IT'S WEIRD, YA KNOW? I was thinking about those newspapers some more, and I keep seeing all these old stories about superheroes from a long time ago and they seem more real.

Gazerbeam and Dynaguy and everyone . . . they all were friends. Like, kind of a family. They were my mom and dad's friends and they all hung out and fought crime. A world where no one was afraid to be a Super. I think maybe my mom and dad might have been . . . I can't even say it . . . cool.

I can't believe I just wrote that, but they really really are kind of . . . Super.

Turns out the guys we got the house from had captured Mom, so Dad was going to rescue her. Then Violet said we should suit up in case trouble happened. Guess what?

Trouble TOTALLY happened!

We were waiting for Frozone to show up. I guess Dad thought something might happen at the house, since the bad guys owned the house and know who we are. And Dad was right because a half dozen hypno-goggle-wearing thugs showed up!

BEST PART NOW ...
READY?!

I TOTALLY had the remote to Dad's old super car. I pressed the summoning button I saw Dad using when he got all mad. AND IT TOTALLY WORKED. Violet, me, and Jack-Jack jumped in the car while Frozone took out the bad guys.

Of course, Mom and Dad were totally over their heads, and Violet and I had to bail them out. I guess Jack-Jack kind of helped too. Lucky Edna had made him that new Supersuit!

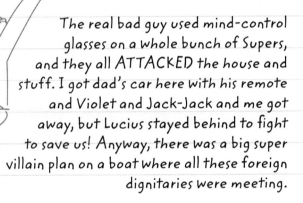

And the pizza guy my mom caught? He was innocent! He was under the control of the Screenslaver!

The real bad guy used mind-control glasses on a whole bunch of Supers, and they all ATTACKED the house and stuff. I got dad's car here with his remote and Violet and Jack-Jack and me got away, but Lucius stayed behind to fight to save us! Anyway, there was a big super villain plan on a boat where all these foreign dignitaries were meeting.

THIS BAD GUY CALLING HIMSELF THE SCREENSLAVER WAS REALLY EVELYN DEAVOR— the younger sister of the guy who loaned us this house! The older brother was innocent. He was mind-controlled by the Screenslaver, too. So, the sister was all being evil and was trying to take over everyone's minds. Jack-Jack, me, and Violet were the only ones not hypnotized. Next thing you know, THERE WAS THIS CRAZY FIGHT AND THE BOAT WENT OUT OF CONTROL.

SUPER FAM!

SAVING THE DAY!

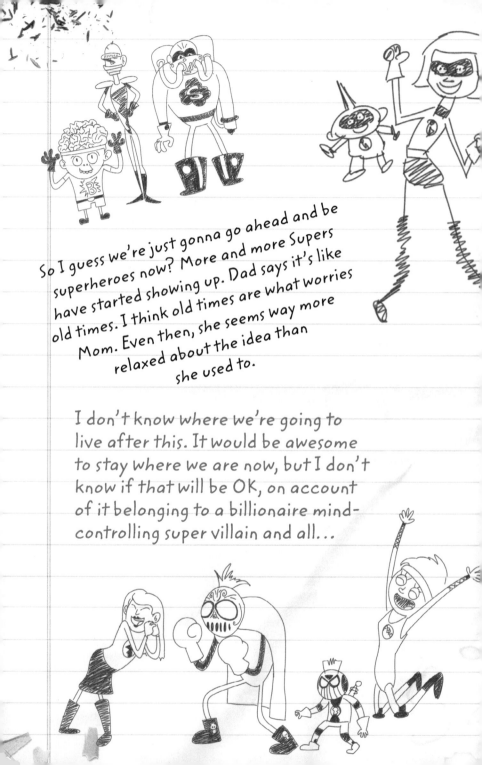

So I guess we're just gonna go ahead and be superheroes now? More and more Supers have started showing up. Dad says it's like old times. I think old times are what worries Mom. Even then, she seems way more relaxed about the idea than she used to.

I don't know where we're going to live after this. It would be awesome to stay where we are now, but I don't know if that will be OK, on account of it belonging to a billionaire mind-controlling super villain and all...

Looking over all the old newspapers and stuff made me think that maybe there should be a new Super team—not just our family, but like, EVERYONE SUPER.

We could all work together in a space station or something, and monitor the world for crimes and bad guys. And then when evil strikes no one will be alone. Not like before where the heroes were hiding and working in secret. That only let bad things happen. That's what I guess matters right? Being with people you trust who can make sure that you're okay.

TEAM LOGO IDEAS

"The League of Supers"

"The Triumphants!"

"The Freedom Brigade"

"The Squad of Safety"

"The Powerhouses"

Aw man. I'm out of pages.

I guess this all proved what I wanted anyway, which is:.

MY DIARY IS WAY MORE INTERESTING THAN VIOLET'S DIARY.

Hers was just boring kissing stuff and clothes and about hating being a Super. Mine is EXCITING and FUN and all about how awesome I am. All books would be better if they talked about how AWESOME I am.

WELL, ANYWAY, THAT'S ALL I HAVE TO WRITE, I THINK. BYE "MATH NOTEBOOK"!

Thanks for being a place I could write cool stuff in!